I0538075

Drawing Dead
A Tale of Poker and Vampires

by Scott McKenzie

Eddie Nelson is a professional poker player, testing his skills in Las Vegas at the World Series of Poker for the first time. Unfortunately, he's on the worst run of his life and can't afford his buy-in to the Main Event. Then he meets a shadowy figure called Raphael who offers to back him for a fifty-fifty split of any winnings. But if he loses, he has to play in a private tournament of Raphael's choosing...

Drawing Dead is a tale of poker and vampires by Scott McKenzie, author of One Day in Gitmo Nation, Death by Autopen and Rebirth.

Copyright © 2014 by Scott McKenzie

ISBN 978-0-9558552-6-9

http://www.stardotfiction.com
Follow *.fiction on Twitter @StarDotFiction

http://www.scottamckenzie.com
Follow the author on Twitter @mckenz1e

Drawing Dead was edited by Rebecca Burruss. Read her blog, Rebecca's Red Pen, at
http://rebeccamhoffman.blogspot.com

About the author

Scott McKenzie lives in Cheshire, UK with his wife and children. With no education in storytelling other than a healthy appetite for fiction in all forms, Scott simply thought he'd see if he could write a novel, then wrote and self-published three in five years. Balancing family, work and a love of sport and movies, Scott writes his fast-paced stories in short sharp bursts.

Also by this author

Rebirth
The Rising
One Day in Gitmo Nation
A Gitmo Nation Christmas Carol
The Foot on the Shore
Death by Autopen

With Phil Ives
Krampus: A Christmas Tale

Introduction

Drawing Dead is a work of fiction. The characters all play the poker variant called Texas Hold 'Em.

Texas Hold 'Em is a variation of the standard card game of poker. Texas Hold 'Em consists of two cards (hole cards) being dealt face down to each player and then five community cards being placed face-up by the dealer—a series of three ("the flop") then an additional single card ("the turn" or "fourth") and another additional card ("the river" or "fifth street")—with players having the option to check, bet, raise, or fold after each deal; i.e., betting may occur prior to the flop, "on the flop", "on the turn", and "on the river".

The intention is to make the best hand of five cards using the seven cards available to you. In ascending order of strength, the hands are:

- High card
- One pair
- Two pair
- Three of a kind
- Straight
- Flush (five cards of the same suit)
- Full house (three of a kind and one pair in the same hand)
- Four of a kind
- Straight flush
- Royal flush (a straight running from ten to ace, all the same suit)

In Texas Hold 'Em, many hands end before each player's cards are revealed, which is to say that most of the time, betting the right amount at the right time, reading your opponents' body language, and making everyone else think you've got the best cards can make the difference between winning and losing. Or, as you're about to find out, it can make the difference between living and dying.

SM, March 2014

1

The incessant sound of riffling poker chips was driving him crazy. The click-click-click of hundreds of poker players rattling chips through their fingers had been an inspiration three days ago, the sound of hope and a collective yearning for the pot of gold at the end of the rainbow. Now it was like Chinese water torture to Eddie Nelson: the never-ending, ever-present sound of boredom, frustration, and anger held barely in check.

This was Eddie's second time in Las Vegas. The first was a three-day jaunt for his twenty-fifth birthday. This time it felt like he'd been here forever and, at times, he wondered whether he'd ever get out of the city alive.

His birthday trip felt like a lifetime ago, but it had been a little over two years, back in the days when a trip to Sin City was a tourist adventure, where the money put down on the tables was the affordable cost of a night's entertainment. But now it was business, and the business Eddie was in was further away from "entertainment" than he ever thought possible.

Eddie folded what felt like the hundredth consecutive hand and checked his watch. It read three-thirty, which could easily have been a.m. or p.m. due to the perpetual insomnia-induced hangover that dogged almost every professional poker player. The uniformed dealer whizzed cards to all nine players seated at the table in his unremarkable mechanical style. In the next half hour, another

3

uncharismatic dealer would take his place, doing nothing to end the monotony except by allowing the players to hear someone say, "Blinds please" in a different voice.

Eddie was on the dealer button, with the small blind and big blind to his left. He watched the other players as they looked at their cards, always testing himself, trying to predict their likely moves by gauging their reactions. The first three folded in quick succession, and the next man round had been sitting with his cards in his hand, almost aiming for the middle of the table before the action moved round to him. Predictably, he folded. The next player raised the bet to four times the big blind and the other players folded round to Eddie, who then and only then looked at his cards.

He was amazed that other players didn't take this approach. Any poker player worth their salt—even amateurs—knows the importance of body language. When you can give away so much information just from the way you look at a pair of cards, why volunteer that information any earlier than you absolutely have to? Surely he wasn't the only one in the tournament looking out for this? This was something Eddie had learned very early on and he had been taking advantage of it ever since. It was one of the golden rules. In blackjack, *always* double down on eleven. In poker, *never* look at your cards until you have to.

He had the king of hearts and the five of clubs. The brief feeling of elation just to be looking at the first face card he'd seen in almost an hour passed in less than a second when he saw the terrible second card and his brain told him to fold. His hands did as they were told, and that was the end of another hand.

Eddie checked one of the dozens of video screens that were dotted around the Rio's massive poker room. Seven hundred players were left in the World Series of Poker Main Event from a starting field of six thousand nine hundred and fifty, who had all started playing almost a week ago. Day "one" was actually split into four days to accommodate all the players and some had entered more than once—re-entering on day 1B after being knocked out on day 1A. Prize money went to the top ten percent of players, so Eddie was doing all he could to grind out a place, playing safe poker and letting the loose players go all-in and knock each other out.

The clock was ticking, though. Only seven players had been knocked out in the last hour and his stack would only cover him for twenty big blinds. Taking into account the antes and one or two cheap calls, he thought he had enough to survive another three or maybe four rotations round the table but when everyone else folded as soon as someone else raised the bet, the rotations were getting quicker and quicker. Time was not on his side.

Shouts echoed around the poker room and the screens changed, indicating that there were six hundred and ninety nine players left. Sarcastic cheers and claps spread from table to table. The dealer finished shuffling the deck and dealt the cards again. Everyone folded round to Eddie. He looked at his cards and tried to conceal his excitement at seeing a pair of aces: hearts and diamonds.

American Airlines.

Bullets.

Pocket rockets.

The screens indicated that another player had dropped out. The common sense part of Eddie's brain told him to fold. He listened to a different voice.

"All in," he announced, pushing his modest stack of chips over the line on the table in front of him. The player on the button folded and he expected the two men on the blinds to follow suit.

5

Even though he didn't have a massive chip stack, his all-in was still a significant over-bet. The small blind folded but the player on the big blind took a couple of seconds to think and then pushed his significantly larger stack of chips over the line.

Eddie hadn't expected his bet to be called. A shiver ran down his spine as he realised that he had put his place in the tournament at risk for the first—and maybe the last—time.

"On your backs," the dealer ordered. Eddie flipped his cards over and watched his opponent wince as he saw the two red aces. Slower than Eddie, he turned over the ace and king of spades. There was a deep intake of breath from everyone around the table. Eddie was easily the favourite to win the hand, but with five cards still to come, he was well aware of the possibility of his opponent hitting a flush of spades, or a queen, jack and ten to hit a straight.

"Good luck," Eddie said, as tradition had been at that table all day when one player was ahead when all the chips had gone in. In the hours to come he would deeply regret uttering those two words.

The dealer went through the motions of dealing three cards into the middle of the table. Each card was a gunshot to Eddie's heart.

Bang! Ten of spades.

Bang! Jack of spades.

Bang! Queen of spades.

The dealer paused before dealing the remaining cards. Everyone at the table looked at each other. Everyone apart from Eddie; he knew he was beaten. A royal flush—the best possible hand—versus a pair of aces. He had no chance of winning the hand. He was out.

A glance up at the screen told him there were six hundred and ninety-seven players left. He heard the words, "He's drawing dead," but stayed at the table until the last two meaningless cards had been dealt.

As he got out of his chair, Eddie shook his opponent's hand and the sound of half-hearted consolation was drowned out as the dealer shouted, "Seat seven empty!" The other players offered their commiserations as Eddie left the table, but he didn't acknowledge them; he was numb. The announcement of "We are now on the bubble" over the PA system confirmed his worst fears—he was the last person to go out of the tournament not to win a prize. Even the person who finished one spot outside the prize places—the "bubble boy"—would be given a free place in next year's tournament, worth ten thousand dollars.

But Eddie was out and had nothing to show for it. Three and a half days had come and gone, with nothing to show for it apart from growing suicidal tendencies and the mother of all headaches. He didn't even bother to try and work out what the odds were of his opponent hitting a royal flush on the flop. It didn't matter anymore; when you were on a bad run, long shots always beat the odds when they were going against you.

Nevada's July sun assaulted him as he stepped out of the air-conditioned casino and onto the strip. Eddie had seen the city a lot busier than it was now in the two months he had been in Las Vegas. One of the reasons the World Series of Poker held an event to attract seven thousand players and all the related journalists, money men, hookers, and other nefarious individuals in the height of summer was the relative lack of tourism during the time when Sin City is hotter than the fires of Hell.

7

He trudged down the strip in a daze, not even noticing the honks from cars as he failed to stop at crossings. The sound of fake Italian singing echoed up from the fake canal below as Eddie made his way up the ramp into the lobby of the Venetian, his home away from home. Inside, the phantom sound of poker chips that had dogged his mind since he left the table was replaced by the banal sound of slot machines. He remembered lying awake with jet lag on his first trip to Vegas with that sound going round and round in his head. He took the elevator up to the thirteenth floor and dragged his feet back to his room. He opened the door and felt something under his foot as he stepped inside.

It was an envelope, addressed with one word: "Eddie." Eddie's pulse quickened as he fumbled to open it. Inside was a postcard with a picture of the Kings and Queens, a casino Eddie had never seen or heard of. He flipped it over. Written in black ink was one word.

Midnight.

2

The last two years had flown past, but so much had happened to Eddie that the events of his old life felt like they belonged to someone else. Growing up in the rainy British city of Manchester, it was only natural for someone with even a passing interest in gambling to yearn for the chance to sample the glamour of Las Vegas, or at least pay a visit to see if it lived up to the glamour of the Ocean's movies.

Of course, the glamour of the movies was Hollywood airbrushing, or at the very least a throwback to the time of the Rat Pack when people hit the tables wearing suits. Now they sat transfixed at video poker machines dressed in hoodies and Crocs, barely muttering a word to another human being and getting as many free drinks as they could before their money ran out, all the while daydreaming about paying off the mortgage with their winnings. Eddie was not a high roller and, with a ten dollar minimum at most tables on the strip, he quickly burned through the five hundred dollars he'd budgeted to gamble during the long weekend away, despite a short run of beginner's luck on the first night. His travelling companion was his girlfriend Karen, and they spent the rest of their trip shopping and taking in a couple of shows

9

until he heard a commotion one night while they were trying to find a route through the maze of slot machines in the Bellagio.

The noise was coming from an area filled with tables where no slot machines could be found, segregated from the rest of the casino floor by a faux stone wall decorated with faux plants and vines. A man in a suit stood at a dais at the entrance. He regarded the inquisitive look on Eddie's face and offered an explanation before Eddie could ask what was going on.

"Please excuse the noise, sir. We have a high stakes game in progress and they're down to the final two players."

"What are they playing?" Karen asked.

"Poker. Texas Hold 'Em." They both stared blankly. The man in the suit continued. "A few hours ago we started with ten players. Each one paid one hundred thousand dollars to sit down at the table."

"How much could they win?" Eddie asked.

"Winner takes all. One million dollars."

Eddie's eyes widened. "But this is Vegas—doesn't the house always win?"

"Not in poker, sir. The house takes a small fee on top of the stake at the beginning but, after that, it's one man against another." Once again, the man spoke in anticipation of Eddie's next question. "You can go in and watch if you want."

Eddie grabbed Karen's hand and led her into the crowd that surrounded the single poker table. Two men with huge piles of multi-coloured chips in front of them were sitting opposite a dealer dressed in black tie. One was a tall guy in a black baseball cap and hockey shirt which both bore the logos of an online poker site. He wore dark shades and had a white Apple earbud stuck in one ear, with the other dangling in front of him. The other player was an overweight man with a head like a potato. He was slumped in his chair and had the look of a pile of clothes with a person stuffed inside. Neither were incredible physical specimens, but here they were, sitting in a room in Vegas playing for more money than almost every major sports star in the world could hope to earn on any single day.

The dealer gave them each two cards. The man with the cap threw some chips in front of him and the other man matched his bet. The dealer then turned three cards face up in the middle of the table—two queens and a four. The man in the cap tapped the table as soon as the third card was revealed and Potato Head took a few seconds to think before pushing all his chips in front of him. Eddie didn't know the rules but somehow, deep within his subconscious, he knew the man in the cap had suckered Potato Head into betting all his chips.

"Call," the man in the cap said immediately in reply and flipped his two cards over. A pair of queens.

Potato Head screamed an obscenity and turned his cards over to reveal a pair of fours. The crowd erupted and the man in the cap punched the air. Eddie heard someone behind him use the phrase "He's drawing dead," which would be something he'd come to hear—and say—a lot over the coming years.

The man in the cap stood up and exchanged high-fives with some people in the crowd as the dealer dealt two more cards face up and then announced, "We have a winner!"

From that moment, Eddie was hooked. He thought of nothing else from the moment he left the Bellagio poker room until he arrived back home in England. He drove Karen crazy on the flight home; every time she tried to talk to him, she had to break him out of his daydream of winning a million dollars just for playing

11

a game of cards. He installed a poker game on his phone before they left and ran his battery dry playing it all the way across the Atlantic.

The way Eddie saw it, poker was the perfect game. It was you against everyone else at the table, not like other casino games where the house always wins in the end. Everyone had an equal shot because the cards were shuffled and dealt fairly and everyone started with the same number of chips. That meant that on any given day, any player could beat any other player, in theory at least.

They got back to their apartment at eight in the evening. Karen announced that she was tired and went straight to bed, but Eddie didn't follow her. He opened his laptop and Googled "online poker," then went to the first site he found. He opened an account, installed the software, and played a few games for play money. He got the hang of calling, raising, and folding against real people and even managed to win a couple of hands by bluffing; betting hard when a king or ace came out and he was sure that whoever he was playing against didn't have either of those cards in their hand. Within an hour, he had doubled the play money he started with.

Eddie reached for his wallet and deposited fifty pounds into his account.

3

Karen woke up and checked her alarm clock. The bright green digits told her it was just after four in the morning, but her mind had a middle-of-the-day alertness. She spent a few minutes lying in bed trying to get back to sleep but quickly resigned herself to the fact that jet lag had taken hold and her body wasn't going to let her sleep any more. The time difference between Las Vegas and Manchester, coupled with the late nights they'd had in Sin City, had thrown her body clock into disarray. She turned over and sat up. When she found an empty space where Eddie should have been, she got out of bed and opened the bedroom door.

The next room was lit only by the light from Eddie's laptop screen, bathing him in blue light as he slept on the sofa. She hit a key on his laptop to get rid of the screensaver, revealing the poker software. She scanned the screen for a few seconds and saw that Eddie had been playing for real money. She read his account balance and took a huge intake of breath, which woke him up.

His look of innocent surprise was quickly replaced by the look of someone who had been caught doing something they shouldn't. He looked at the screen, then at Karen, who had her hand over her mouth.

"What have you done, Eddie?" she said.

13

"I wasn't tired when you went to bed so I thought I'd have a go at playing poker."

"But why have you got more than four hundred pounds in your account? You know how hard we saved for this holiday."

"I won it."

"What, all of it?"

"Well, I started with twenty," he lied.

"You made nearly four hundred pounds? How long were you playing for?"

I won all this money, Eddie thought. *I won it for* us. *Why is she so angry?*

"Four or five hours, I think. I lost track of time."

She stood over him, torn between the discovery of Eddie's new-found talent and the fact that he'd spent so much time playing poker instead of coming to bed with her. The money he spent wasn't the issue—not this time anyway. She said nothing, and it spoke volumes.

"Come on, let's go to bed," he said.

"I've been to bed," she said. "I'm not tired any more. I'm going to read for a while. You go to bed."

There was no warmth in her voice; that was an order. Eddie knew immediately that the money he won was outweighed by his absence, to Karen at least. When he looked back, Eddie always thought of the night they got back from Vegas as the beginning of the end. It wasn't just the beginning of the end of their relationship, though; it was the end of life as he knew it.

From that day onward, everything he had known before went out the window. Poker was everything. As he stayed up later and later to play poker online, he lost his bearings on reality. He struggled to fit his workday into his new schedule and took the initiative to leave before he was sacked, which his boss told him was only days away when he handed in his resignation. Eddie didn't care; he was confident in his abilities as a poker player and, as he hoped, the winnings from his first month of playing online poker full-time exceeded his old monthly wage by almost fifty percent.

With money in the bank and a healthy stake to play with, he decided to try playing in a live tournament. He found a casino just outside the city centre that hosted a tournament every Saturday afternoon. With an entry fee of just ten pounds, it attracted a lot of amateur players who looked forward to the game all week at work. Eddie was different. His life was one long weekend and poker was no longer the hobby that gobbled up his disposable income; it was business to him now. Did he win every single tournament he entered? Of course not, but his life had become one long game rather than a series of intermittent attempts to win big. That said, he regularly made the final table from a field of over a hundred players and he quickly tired of the relative lack of challenge. He also knew he was ready to play for higher stakes, both online and in the real world.

He took a train across the Peak District to Nottingham, home of Dusk Till Dawn, one of the biggest poker venues in the UK. Every month they hosted a tournament with a guaranteed prize pot of two hundred thousand pounds, which cost five hundred pounds to enter. With around thirty percent of the pot going to the ultimate winner, the chance of walking out of a club seventy grand richer drew the best players from all over the country. After busting out by playing too loose too early in his first tournament, Eddie went back home and played in every live tournament he could find. He began to understand the differences between playing fast and loose online where you can play hands every few seconds and

15

playing in live tournaments, where most hands take a few minutes to play out. He changed his approach to every game and realised how the way he played and the things he said had a psychological effect on his opponents.

Eddie returned to Dusk Till Dawn a month later and made the final table, finished in second place, and walked out of the club as the sun was rising with a five figure bundle of cash overflowing from his pockets. As he lay awake at five a.m. in his bed in a budget hotel room situated in a dull grey industrial estate, the images of cards and the sound of riffling poker chips buzzed around his brain.

I've got a stake now, he thought as he looked at the piles of fifty pound notes wrapped in red plastic sitting on the bedside table. *It's time to head back to Vegas.*

4

The World Series of Poker is an annual festival of the world's favourite card game. Beginning in May, the Rio casino resort hosts fifty-seven tournaments taking in many variations of the game, with buy-ins beginning at one thousand dollars and stretching into the high five figures. The big one—the tournament every player in the world from the home-game dreamer to the seasoned pro wants to win—is event fifty-seven, the ten thousand dollar no-limit Texas Hold 'Em event, referred to solely as "the Main Event". Played in July every year, the Main Event attracts upwards of six thousand players, offering a prize pot of over sixty million dollars, which can result in an eight figure prize for the winner.

Eddie left Manchester on a plane in May, with a return seat booked for the end of July. After he'd negotiated and paid up front for a ten-week stay at the Venetian, he had a stake of twenty thousand pounds, or around thirty thousand dollars. He started off slow, ignoring the first few tournaments of the World Series and opting to play low stakes house tournaments at casinos up and down the strip. It gave him a feel for the place, one that he didn't get when he'd visited Vegas with his now ex-girlfriend. He saw the same faces across the table again and again and could easily pick out the professionals from the tourists, who rarely had a chance.

17

Without a word or barely a look at each other, the professionals collectively bullied the tourists to make sure their money remained in Sin City long after they had flown back to their wives and office jobs.

But this was Eddie's job. Within a week of stepping off the plane, he was grinding out more than enough from daily tournaments and cash games to cover meals, drinks, and the next day's stake. Then he was making enough to cover some entertainment, too. He set himself a budget and stuck to it. He wasn't pulling in hookers-and-blow money, but on a good day it covered a growing interest in Jack Daniel's and strippers.

When his stake crept up to forty thousand dollars, he thought it was time for him to sign up for a chance to win a World Series bracelet and paid three thousand dollars for his seat at a no-limit tournament with about five hundred other players. He made it through day one of the three day event—but only just—and walked away from his table less than an hour into day two. He chastised himself—occasionally out loud—all the way down the strip, walked immediately into a cash game at Planet Hollywood and lost another two thousand dollars in less than an hour. From that moment, Eddie learned what it meant when he heard professionals talk about "going on tilt".

Day after day he played more and more games, walking away too early from no-limit tournaments and too late from high stakes cash games. Forty thousand dollars can stretch a long way in most cities all over the world, but not in Vegas, especially when you're on a bad run and there's no one around to tell you to stop.

When he had little more than ten thousand dollars left two weeks before the Main Event, he had a decision to make: register for the World Series and stop playing for a couple of weeks or push

18

on and then register when the bank roll was back up to what he'd started with.

Eddie made a bad call. A week later, the money was gone. As he got up from his final cash game and walked to the bar, it hit him that he had almost a month to wait until his flight home. At that moment, the allure of Vegas disappeared. He was stuck in a city that exists solely to take the money out of your pocket and he had no money left. The house had won.

He took a seat at the bar, waving away the approaching bartender as he called the airline on his mobile phone. They said it would cost an additional two hundred and fifty pounds to change his flight; two hundred and fifty pounds he didn't have. He hung up and started to flick through his contacts to work out which one of the few friends he had left back home would lend him the money, but before he could hit the call button, someone took the stool next to him.

"Tough beat. Can I buy you a drink?" the stranger asked.

Eddie turned to look at his visitor. The man was dressed in a black suit with an open-neck white shirt. Eddie estimated his age at mid-twenties but, when he regarded his face, he saw that the eyes held the wisdom of someone much older.

"Sure, why not," Eddie replied, shrugging in the way someone can only when they realise they have absolutely nowhere in the entire world to go at that moment in time.

The stranger beckoned the bartender over. "Wild Turkey, no ice. And..." He turned to Eddie.

"Seeing as it's not even midday yet, I'll go with a beer," Eddie said. "Coors on draft in the biggest glass you've got."

"You got it," the bartender said.

The stranger laughed. "You know, I didn't realise what time it was. You must be on a bad run."

"What makes you say that?" Eddie asked.

"No one who's on a streak in Vegas cares what time of day it is."

Eddie thought back to when Lady Luck had been on his side. "I guess you're right."

The drinks arrived. The stranger threw a twenty the bartender's way and told him to keep the change. They clinked glasses and Eddie took a long pull on his beer. He said, "Well, you've bought me a drink so I'd better ask your name. I'm Eddie."

He held out his hand and the stranger shook it. "Call me Raphael," he said. The stranger's turn of phrase felt a little odd, but Eddie put it down to his own incredible exhaustion and thought nothing more of it.

"I saw that last hand," Raphael said. "Like I said, tough beat. You were pretty much drawing dead from the flop."

"Pretty much. That's been the story for the last two weeks. You should have seen me before then—it was a different story." Eddie took another swig of beer and traced a drip of condensation down the glass with his finger.

"I did."

Eddie looked up from his beer to see a sly smile on Raphael's face. "You did what?"

"See you. I've been watching you play since you got here."

Eddie looked around the bar. He suddenly didn't feel as lonely as he had just minutes earlier, but not in a good way.

"What do you mean, you've been watching me since I got here?"

The stranger leaned in. "There are many of us, up and down the strip. We watch everyone who plays poker, especially in the run-up to the Main Event."

"Well, you can forget about me. I won't be playing in the Main Event."

"That's why I'm here. I want to stake you."

It took a few seconds for the stranger's proposal to register. "You want to stake me?" Eddie said. "Why? It's ten thousand dollars and you've just seen me bust out like a total amateur. If you've been watching me long enough, you'll know I've been on tilt for weeks."

"Yes, I've been watching you long enough. But I can see you've got potential."

Eddie finished his beer with one massive chug and pushed the glass away. "What's the catch?"

Without a pause for breath, Raphael said, "I get fifty percent of any winnings."

"A ten thousand dollar bet on a one-in-ten chance of me finishing in the money, maybe one in a hundred that I'll win decent money—all for a fifty-fifty split? There's got to be a catch. What if I bust out?"

"Then you play in a private tournament for me."

There's the rub, Eddie thought. The bartender reappeared and Raphael didn't ask Eddie if he wanted another drink. "Same again for both of us," he said.

"What kind of private tournament?" Eddie asked.

"It's a secret. High stakes, but you won't have to put any money down. You don't need to worry about it, though. Finish in the money and we both get paid. Finish outside the money and you do me a favour. What do you say?"

21

The second round of drinks arrived. Eddie watched the tiny wisps of mist from the frosted glass dancing in the air. He grabbed the glass, took a swig of the beer he didn't have enough money to pay for, and considered his options.

5

"Where to, buddy?" the driver asked as Eddie got into the taxi in the neon-flooded night outside the Venetian.

Eddie flashed the postcard at the taxi driver. "Kings and Queens Casino. Do you know it?"

With an ominous smile, he replied, "Oh, yeah, I know it." Eddie didn't like the taxi driver's tone.

He felt like Alice falling down the rabbit hole. His future was a blank canvas. He was sitting in a cab taking him somewhere unknown to see someone he barely knew to play poker with God knows who for God knows what stakes. He had lost ten thousand dollars of someone else's money and now he was about to repay that debt in ways he was trying not to imagine.

The cab headed up the strip toward Fremont Street but took a left turn, then another left, then a right, and Eddie lost his bearings as the lights of the super casinos faded into the distance behind them. Eddie knew he was definitely off the strip when the street lights ended and the cab was plunged into darkness. Eddie leaned forward to talk to the driver, who anticipated his question.

"Don't worry, buddy," he said into his rear view mirror, "we're nearly there."

The ride continued for another couple of minutes until the taxi came to a stop in a parking lot.

"Journey's end, buddy."

Eddie looked out of the window. It was dark all around him. "I thought you were taking me to a casino?" he said.

"I did," the taxi driver said, waving his thumb at the blackness outside. "It's out there, on the other side of the lot."

Eddie sighed and asked how much he owed the driver for the ride.

"Not a thing. I've got a deal with the owners."

"But you just picked me up off the street. How..."

"We've *all* got a deal with the owners. Good luck, buddy."

No sooner had Eddie stepped out of the cab than it sped away into the darkness. As his eyes adjusted, a black shape formed at the opposite end of the parking lot. Standing three stories high, the Kings and Queens was tiny compared to the Venetian or the Bellagio. The sign above the entrance doors was a faded and peeling representation of the classic face cards, a king and a queen. Eddie wondered how many years, or how many decades, had passed since this casino last hosted genuine paying customers. He walked across the parking lot and up the steps to the entrance, the crumbling tarmac and dirt crunching underfoot. The warm desert breeze blew ancient litter and the detritus of an abandoned facility around him.

He stopped at the top of the steps and turned at the distant sound of an engine to see a pair of headlights winding its way through the dusty roads in his direction. It was another cab, which stopped in the same place where Eddie had been dropped off and another man got out, who looked as confused and apprehensive as Eddie assumed he had just a minute earlier.

24

"Good evening, Eddie," said a voice from over his shoulder. Eddie spun on his heels and came face-to-face with Raphael, in the same suit and shirt combination he had been wearing when they first met at the bar after he busted out.

"I'm glad you could make it. Come in and meet the other players."

6

Raphael led Eddie through the decaying lobby, with peeling walls and stains dried into every surface, and into the casino's main gaming room. The scene before him looked like the remnants of a frantic evacuation from long ago. The chips and cards of unfinished games remained on the tables. Overturned stools and smashed glasses were scattered all over the filthy carpet. It looked as if the casino's last customers had jumped to their feet and scrambled for the door, without thinking about leaving tall stacks of chips behind.

They worked their way through the remains of the casino to a door at the end of the room. Raphael opened it to reveal a single poker table sitting in the middle of what Eddie assumed used to be the room where high rollers would hold private, high stakes games. Seven men sat round the table. Some were young, some were old, but all of them had the same look on their faces, all silently screaming, *How the hell did I end up here?*

Behind each seat stood another man, each dressed the same as Raphael in a black suit and white shirt. There were three empty seats, two for extra poker players and one for the dealer. Raphael motioned for Eddie to sit down in one of the empty chairs. He did so, then watched as the final player walked through the door accompanied by another man in a suit and took the final empty seat.

The door opened for a final time and another man in a suit, differentiated from the others only by his black bow tie, sat down in the dealer's seat. On the table in front of him, a deck of cards had been laid out face up, with each suit in order from two to ace. With well-practiced flair, the dealer flipped the cards over and began to shuffle. As he did so, he broke the uncomfortable silence that hung over the room.

"The game is no-limit Texas Hold 'Em. You each have ten thousand in chips in front of you. The blinds start at twenty-five and fifty." The dealer dealt one card face up to each player. Eddie was dealt a king, the highest card anyone received, and the dealer threw a thick plastic button marked "Dealer" in front of him and continued talking. "Blinds go up every twenty minutes."

With that explanation, Eddie felt some semblance of reality descend on the room. The scene had become a little more familiar; this tournament had a fairly standard structure.

The player to the dealer's left asked, "What are we playing for?"

Without looking up from shuffling the cards, the dealer replied, "You all received a stake from one of our representatives and you all failed to return on that investment. That is why you are playing in this tournament—for our entertainment."

"But what are the prizes?"

"You don't need to know right now. That will become clear as the game progresses." The dealer then looked up at the players to Eddie's left and said, "Blinds please, gentlemen."

That was it. No pleasantries, no complimentary drinks served by wannabe models, no idea what they were playing for, and a deep, intense collective feeling that they had no choice. They threw their chips in front of them and the game began.

27

7

"Blinds are now fifty and one hundred," the dealer said.

Eddie looked at his opponents. Some of them riffled chips through their fingers, others were watching the action intently, but they all had the same amount of chips in front of them; none of them had played a hand. For twenty straight minutes everyone to the left of the big blind had folded, leaving that player to take the chips down. It wasn't surprising; after all, none of them knew what they were playing for. As far as Eddie could tell, none of them knew each other either so they didn't even have bragging rights to play for.

Eddie was on the dealer button again. Everyone round from the big blind folded, then he looked at his cards. Ace of clubs and ace of spades.

American Airlines.

Bullets.

Pocket rockets.

Whether you're playing for a million or a penny, you've got to play aces.

"I raise," he announced, which got a reaction from everyone at the table, including the dealer. "Three hundred," he said, and threw the chips in front of him. The other two players insta-folded but, at long last, someone had made a move. This had a knock-on effect on the rest of the players and every hand on the next rotation of the table involved at least one raise and a couple of hands went all the way to the end, with players turning their cards over.

But the game remained friendly and no one made a point of value betting or trying to put a fellow player all-in. The room would have had the air of a home game, were it not for the men in suits standing in silence behind each player.

Eddie had once read about how zoologists study the habits of animals in captivity. The first time they set foot in the cage, the animals would be aware of their presence and would react as if they were a threat or beg for food, depending on the relationships they may have already established. But day after day, the attention given to the zoologists would wane until they were ignored completely. At this point, the animals began to behave as if they weren't being watched and the study could begin.

Eddie didn't think about this at all while he was playing poker in the private room at the Kings and Queens casino, but had he done so, he would have noticed a striking similarity. All nine players became engrossed in their game, raising and re-raising each other while keeping the atmosphere friendly and exchanging banter based on their perceptions of each others' playing style. They became lost in the game, oblivious to the fact that none of them knew what they were playing for.

When the blinds went up to two hundred and four hundred, the players with short stacks were beginning to feel the pinch as the play moved around the table to them. Eddie found himself on the button again and noticed that the players to his left had very short stacks as they threw their blinds across the line. The big blind examined the modest stack that stood before him.

"May as well go all in," he said, as he threw the rest of his chips into the middle. He was raising the bet out of turn but the dealer said nothing. The players between him and Eddie all folded. After a couple of decent hands, Eddie was sitting on a stack of almost fifteen thousand. He looked at the small blind's stack—it wasn't much more than two thousand so without looking at his cards he raised to three thousand to force the small blind to think about going all in.

"Yeah, why not?" the small blind said, and threw his chips in.

"On your backs," the dealer said, and the players all flipped their cards over.

Eddie had the eight and nine of spades. The small blind had red fours and the big blind had the king of clubs and jack of diamonds. The flop came out three-six-five, all different suits. The owner of the pair of fours perked up: he was still ahead and had more options to improve his hand further. The turn card was a king. The big blind breathed a sigh of relief and then immediately hid behind his fist with the phrase "Please God, give me a blank card on the river" written all over his face.

The river card was a seven. The small blind jumped up and shouted "Yes!" in reaction to having hit his straight from three to seven, then sat back down and sighed, "Oh, no" as he realised Eddie had hit a higher straight: five to nine. The big blind hung his head as Eddie collected the chips from the middle of the table.

Silence descended over the room. The great unspoken question by everyone was, *What happens to these people now that they've lost all their chips?* The faces of the two men who had lost all their chips turned white and the other players all exchanged worried glances. All at once they realised they had been playing without any

30

idea of what they were playing for and only now did they start to think about what they might lose.

The next few seconds were a blur to Eddie, but when they were over, he had no doubt about the seriousness of the trap he had fallen into.

8

The first thing he saw was the heads of the losing players jerk back in unison. Then came the most unholy sound he had ever heard: a cacophony of crunching, tearing, and gurgling. The losers' bodies disappeared into the dark void behind them and their screams of terror were quickly silenced. Something sprayed out of the darkness; as soon as it caught the light, Eddie knew it was blood. The dark red felt of the poker table masked the droplets, but as the blood splattered on their playing cards, the sight of scarlet on white glinting in the low light confirmed what they all feared: the two men were dead.

Seven pairs of eyes darted around the room, seeking comfort from each other but desperately not wanting to get that final confirmation from another person that this was actually happening. All but one of the players sat frozen in their chairs. The player to Eddie's right was breathing heavily, almost hyperventilating, and rocking backward and forward. He was mumbling something to himself, which became audible, then got louder and louder.

"This isn't happening. This isn't happening. This isn't happening."

He repeated his mantra over and over until it reached a crescendo and he jumped up, threw his chair back, and made a run for the door. Before his hand could reach the door handle, there was a deafening bang and the side of his head exploded in a massive burst of blood, brains, and shattered skull fragments, splattering gore all over the walls. His inert body collapsed to the ground and the sudden silence of the room went unnoticed behind the ringing in everyone's ears.

Within the smoke that now filled the room, the suited man that had been standing behind the escapee's seat slowly walked toward the dead body. Eddie caught the sight of a gleaming silver handgun being holstered beneath his suit jacket. The man bent down and groaned, "I always get the runners."

The man in the suit opened his mouth wide—wider than Eddie thought possible—and sunk his teeth into the gaping wound in the dead man's skull. Despite the smoke from the gunshot obscuring his vision, Eddie watched in disgusted horror as the suited man drank the blood of the dead man as the final spasms of life ebbed away. Eddie heard one of the other players throwing up, but he couldn't turn away. He was transfixed by the scene before him: the most horrific, disturbing, and surreal thing he had ever seen in his life. As the man in the suit continued to feed, the murderers of the other two victims returned to their places behind the now-empty seats.

The dealer reached across the table and gathered the blood-soaked playing cards together. He arranged them in a neat pile and placed them out of sight under the table, retrieving a blood-stained towel that had clearly been used many times for the same purpose. He stood up, leaned over the table, and mopped up the patches of blood. With no further thought, as if the scene before him was just another day at the office, he took another deck of cards out of his pocket and started to shuffle them. The man who had been feeding on the runner reached over the table and removed the chips he had been playing with.

There were deep intakes of breath from everyone. The man's face was caked with blood. His white shirt was now stained red. With the sleeve of his suit jacket, he wiped his mouth and smiled, revealing his extended canine teeth. Despite everything they knew—or thought they knew—about the world they lived in, they were suddenly shown a glimpse of the real world, a world where vampires existed.

The dealer made an announcement. "For those of you who haven't worked out the rules, they are as follows. You're playing no-limit Texas Hold 'Em. This is a winner-takes-all game. When you go out of the tournament, you are food for your sponsor. That is the price of your sponsorship. Had you all finished in the money at the Main Event, the two of you would be enjoying your cut of the winnings and you would be none the wiser. But you didn't finish in the money and now you are party to one of the great secrets of your world."

The dealer fell silent for a moment to let the information sink in. He saw the look on their faces, the look he had seen countless times before. Here were six men who had only just met each other and they all knew that five of them would die before... Well, before what? The dealer continued.

"I'll save you from asking me the question that you are undoubtedly asking yourselves. There is a prize for the winner of the tournament, but that will only be revealed at the end. Oh, and if you're wondering whether your friends will rise from the dead as vampires themselves, don't worry. This isn't Hollywood. They're dead—end of story. Any questions?"

Once again, there was silence as the dealer finished shuffling the cards. He looked at the mountain of chips in the middle of the table, then looked at Eddie.

"You won that hand. They're your chips."

Eddie reached over the table and, with shaking hands, dragged the chips toward him.

"Okay," the dealer said, "let's play poker."

9

Eddie was on the big blind. He watched four players look at their cards and fold them all the way round to the player on his right. The player on the small blind was wearing a green polo shirt bearing the logo of an online casino, sunglasses, and a black baseball cap. Eddie was sure he knew all of the major professionals who were sponsored by the online casinos and he didn't know who this guy was. Maybe he was an up-and-coming player, or maybe he was just trying to make everyone believe he was a professional player by wearing a shirt that anyone could pick up for a few dollars or a few thousand loyalty points.

The small blind looked at his cards, then immediately looked at his stack of chips. Then he looked at Eddie's stack, which he was still arranging into piles of twenty-five, hundred, and five-hundred chips.

He's got a strong hand, Eddie thought as he compared their stacks. With his winnings from the last hand, Eddie thought he had him covered by about three to one.

"All in," the small blind said, and pushed all his chips over the line.

The other four players shifted in their seats. Eddie knew what they were thinking; he would be thinking exactly the same if he was one of them.

Knock him out, then I'll be one place closer to winning.

Eddie thought about his situation for a moment while he continued stacking his chips. He hadn't looked at his cards yet but he knew right away that he was in a weak position. One, he was still stacking his winnings from the last hand. That is always a bad time to make a decision about calling an all-in; you might have fewer chips than you thought. Two, if Eddie had his chip counts right, the guy in the green shirt would be back on an even keel if he won the hand. Three, surely no one would go all-in with a weak hand, knowing their life was on the line.

Eddie mucked his cards without looking at them. The guy in the green shirt smiled and said, "You're all cowards!"

He flipped his cards over to reveal the two of clubs and the seven of diamonds. Two-seven off-suit: mathematically, that was the worst possible hand you could be dealt in Texas Hold 'Em. Only a maniac or someone with a point to prove went all-in with a hand like that.

Eddie looked at the other players and realised the guy in green did have a point to prove—they all did—and he had made his move first. The guy in green had decided to play exactly how the professionals say you should play when you're "on the bubble", when you're on the verge of knocking someone out of the tournament so everyone else can finish in the money. You're not supposed to sit back and wait for the other players to knock each other out—you push on, playing every hand aggressively, regardless of which two cards you have been dealt.

That was how Eddie should have played in the Main Event, but no, he let himself get blinded off until he didn't have enough chips left to make a stand.

The guy in the green shirt added Eddie's big blind chips to his modest stack and looked each player in the eye, one by one.

"I don't know about you guys," he began, "but I came to Vegas to play poker. I'm sure everyone sitting at this table thinks they're the best player at any table on any given day. Well, now's the chance for one of us to prove it. One of us is going to bring their A-game today. Maybe there will be one of us left to tell the tale, maybe not, but I say fuck these bloodsuckers. We're probably all dead men anyway, so let's play like it's our last game. I guess the good news is that if we make a bad call or a bad raise, we won't be kicking ourselves for long. What do you say?"

Everyone around the table exchanged glances. Eddie shrugged and spoke first. "I'm with you. Let's play."

The other players nodded and sounded their agreement.

"Right then," the guy in green continued with a smile on his face, "that'll be a buck each."

"What are you talking about?" the player to the right of the dealer said.

Eddie laughed and reached for his wallet. He took out a dollar bill and threw it across the table to the guy in green. "Two-seven off-suit, right?"

The guy in green nodded.

"What does that mean?" the player to the right of the dealer asked.

"Home game rules," said Eddie. "Two-seven-off is the worst hand you can have, so if you win a hand with those cards, everyone else has to give you a dollar."

The other four players made a motion as if they were going to protest, then realised the absurdity of the situation they found themselves in.

"Just trying to lighten the mood, guys," the man in green said.

They all dug out their wallets and threw their dollar bills across the table. The dealer collected the cards and shuffled the deck.

"Blinds please," he said as he dealt the next hand.

10

For the first time in the game, Eddie made a point of taking notice of his opponents, and kicked himself for not having done so earlier. To his right was the maniac in the green shirt, who he now had a good handle on. To his left was an overweight man who looked like he was in his late forties or early fifties, but Eddie knew that he could easily be younger than that; playing poker in dark rooms all day was not conducive to a good diet or pride in one's personal appearance.

The next player round the table was a really young guy, barely old enough to enter the casinos of Las Vegas. He was stick thin, his black- and white-striped designer shirt hanging off him like it had been dropped on a wooden pole. Eddie recognised him; he was a young professional player who had made the leap into major live tournaments on the back of his online play. An online casino had put him on their payroll and Eddie had seen TV coverage of tournaments he played. He was a major draw, playing fast and loose and trash-talking his opponents in a way that made him compelling to watch. Now it was a different story. The action was on him and his hands were shaking as he mucked his cards. He was close to tears and Eddie wondered if this was the first time in his life when he had truly felt out of his depth. The confidence of being young, rich, and unbeatable meant nothing when you were facing the likely prospect of being killed by a vampire on the turn of a card.

The action moved to his left, to another older man, probably in his forties, who was wearing a suit jacket with an open-neck white shirt. He had well-coiffured salt and pepper hair and he did not look like someone who had to play with other peoples' money. He looked at his cards, thought for a moment, and folded.

The final stranger at the table was short-stacked and faced the prospect of losing most of chips in the rotation of the blinds within the next few hands. He was probably in his mid-thirties and Eddie immediately had him down as a long-time professional. He didn't recognise the man's face, but Eddie knew that with only two years' experience in the poker scene, there were thousands of people grinding out a living playing poker—and many more struggling to grind out a living—that he had never heard of. He looked at his cards, then covered his face with his hands in obvious exasperation and mumbled "All in" through his fingers.

Green Shirt folded, then Eddie looked at his cards.

Six and seven of spades.

"How much have you got?" Eddie asked Thirtysomething.

After a few seconds of organising his chips, he said "Two thousand three hundred."

Eddie had over thirty thousand in chips, but he looked at Fat Man to his left and saw that he was sitting on a pile of about fifteen thousand. He wasn't prepared to put that much at risk for low suited connectors so he folded.

Fat Man called and they flipped their cards over. Thirtysomething had a pair of jacks and Fat Man had a king and a queen.

41

"We've got a race," the dealer said. Their chances of winning the hand were close to fifty-fifty, but the low pair was winning before the flop.

"I'm not dead yet," Thirtysomething said, laughing nervously. He received only polite, reluctant smiles in return. Even his opponent, who would usually offer him "good luck" due to his massive deficit in chips, remained silent.

The flop came ace, seven, six.

Shit! Eddie thought to himself as he saw that he had thrown away an instant two pair on the flop.

The turn card was a ten. No change in situation for anyone; the pair of jacks was still ahead.

The river card was another ace. The pair of jacks held up and Thirtysomething collected his chips. He'd doubled up but was still the short stack at the table. "I live to fight another day," he said with a nervous smirk.

Eddie noted that the ace on the river would have counterfeited his pair of sixes. Had he played his six and seven, his strongest hand would have been two pair: aces and sevens. He would have beaten Fat Man though, and would have knocked him out if he had called Eddie's all-in. That decision had meant the difference between life and death and Eddie realised that every single decision he made had the potential to end anyone's life, not just his own.

It was then that Eddie had a revelation. He had just learned that vampires truly do exist in the world, but these vampires were not hiding in coffins, waiting on their human slaves to bring them sacrificial virgins. Maybe these vampires were just the equivalent of regular schmucks who liked playing poker—regular schmucks like him. Maybe they had played poker before they turned into

42

vampires. Wait a minute—were these vampires even human once or were they born that way? He told himself he should forget what he thought he knew from the movies. He was trapped in this room, forced to play poker like Robert De Niro's character was forced to play Russian Roulette in The Deer Hunter. He wanted to ask his captors so many questions, but decided to keep them to himself. For now, at least.

11

Everyone folded the next few hands until the blinds went up again to four hundred and eight hundred. Thirtysomething was clearly anxious about the big blind working its way round to him; eight hundred was a significant percentage of his remaining stack. It was no surprise when he announced that he was all in for the second time. Green Shirt folded and Eddie looked at his cards: a pair of sixes. He would have preferred to be in control of the game when playing a hand like that, so he folded.

Fat Man had more chips than Thirtysomething and went all in over the top, wanting everyone else at the table to know that he had a strong hand and may as well have told everyone else to fold. They all did. No one liked being all in with more than one opponent; there were too many variables and always a chance for an outsider to hit a fluke pair or three of a kind. The pot in the middle of the table was about ten thousand chips when they flipped their cards over. Either Thirtysomething would be back to his starting stack, leaving Fat Man short stacked, or Thirtysomething was dead and Fat Man would close in on Eddie's chip count.

Thirtysomething winced as they saw each other's cards. He had ace eight; Fat Man had ace ten and was the firm favourite to win the hand. Thirtysomething held his head in his hands as the

44

dealer dealt the flop, which came out five-seven-four, then he perked up. A six would give him a straight from five to nine. Neither of them had options for a flush so a six was the card that could save his life.

"Did anyone fold a six?" Thirtysomething asked, looking at everyone one by one.

"I did," Skinny and Green Shirt said in unison, both immediately regretting it. Skinny said he had folded six-two; ten-six for Green Shirt. Thirtysomething saw his slim chances cut in half.

Eddie did everything he could not to look at Thirtysomething, but their eyes met. The hope in Thirtysomething's face drained away in an instant. Sometimes you know, just *know,* without any doubt whatsoever, which two cards another person has, or *had* in Eddie's case. Thirtysomething looked at the flop cards again. Now only an eight gave him a chance.

The dealer turned over the turn card. It was a ten.

Everyone around the table knew only a six could save him now, but Eddie and he both knew that there were no sixes left in the deck. He was drawing dead.

Thirtysomething stood up and said "Good luck" to everyone at the table, then turned round to face his sponsor before the river card was dealt. It was a two, but it didn't matter; he was already dead.

A pair of unseen hands grabbed his shirt and dragged him screaming into the smoky darkness behind the table.

12

There were three deaths on the next hand, which was dealt while the disgusting sounds of ripping and slurping could still be heard behind the place where Thirtysomething had been sitting just moments ago. There were five players left: Eddie was the chip leader, but only just; Fat Man was a close second; Green shirt was sitting on about twenty thousand; White Shirt was next with about seven thousand; and Skinny was now the short stack with about five thousand.

White Shirt took out a silver-coloured hip flask and took a swig. The dealer glared at him.

"We're okay to drink, right?" he said, to which the dealer shrugged in a gesture of "I guess so."

"Anyone else want a hit?" White Shirt asked, brandishing his hip flask. "It's not like we have to worry about dying of liver failure."

Fat Man and Green Shirt waved the offer away, as did Eddie. He never drank when he played poker; he always wanted to keep a clear head. Alcohol made him impulsive and more likely to take unnecessary risks, something he had learned in his early days of playing live tournaments.

Skinny was sitting next to White Shirt and accepted his offer. He took a big gulp from the flask and screwed his face up as he swallowed it.

"Holy shit," he croaked, "what the hell is that?"

"My own special recipe," White Shirt said, then he took another swig and put the flask back in his suit pocket.

The dealer followed the action round the table. White Shirt had the dealer button, which meant that Thirtysomething's seat was the small blind, but he was out so there were no chips in his place. In a regular game, which would be referred to as a "dead small blind" but in a show of vampiric sensitivity, the dealer didn't mention it. Green Shirt was the big blind and looked at his cards as soon as they were dealt. It was Eddie's move. Out of the corner of his eye he could see Green Shirt's hands poised over his chips. *He's ready to push them in*, he thought.

He looked at his cards—an eight and a three—and breathed a sigh of relief that he had an easy decision to make. He folded. Fat Man folded and Skinny pushed all in, giving away the lack of strength of his hand with the announcement, "Good luck guys, been great knowing you."

White Shirt folded and Green Shirt instantly called. He had Skinny covered and was only putting about a quarter of his chip stack at risk.

They flipped their cards over. Skinny revealed a pair of fives and Green Shirt had an ace and a queen. The dealer dealt the flop, which came out ace-king-seven. Skinny shook his head, but the look on his face from the moment he'd gone all in had told everyone he thought he was already a dead man. The turn card was another seven and an ace came out on the river.

47

Skinny had barely registered the fact that the pair of fives he had been dealt didn't even play when his sponsor grabbed him and dragged him backwards. The screams of agony as the vampire sunk its teeth into the losing player's neck hadn't lost any of the horror, but it was no longer a surprise. To the four players now left at the table, the penalty for losing was quickly becoming a normal occurrence to them.

But what they weren't expecting was a second scream, this time from someone else. Someone who sounded like they were in even more pain than the poor kid having the blood drained from this neck. Eddie, Fat Man, and Green Shirt all exchanged "What the hell is going on?" looks and saw White Shirt taking another swig from his hip flask. He raised the flask in a *cheers* salute to the vampires that ringed the table, then there was an enormous gunshot noise and the centre of his chest blew open in a massive explosion of gore.

"Nobody move," came a voice from the darkness behind Eddie. He didn't need to be told that Raphael was the one who had just killed White Shirt, and he would be the one to kill the rest of them if they didn't comply.

The other vampires rushed to gather around the space that Skinny's body had disappeared into. The screaming continued, and in the commotion, Eddie heard the words *poison, bloodstream,* and *undercover.* Then, all of a sudden, the screaming ended and the other vampires fell silent. There was a crackling, sizzling sound and a plume of dust was carried into the air. Dark grey smoke filled the air, then dissipated. The vampires whispered amongst themselves.

"I had my suspicions about him."

"Why didn't you stop him drinking from the flask?"

"I should have shot him there and then."

The vampires all took their positions. The dealer saw the dumbfounded looks on the faces of the three remaining players, shuffled the cards, and spoke.

"The looks on your faces tell me that you have no idea what happened. I'll ask you all: did you have anything to do with that?"

All three players shook their heads.

"Good. You should know that we will be tracking down this man's family and making them pay the price for his treachery. The man he killed had been with us for over a hundred years. He was one of the best we had at finding talent for our games, but he made a mistake, which proved fatal. Be warned: the same fate will fall on your families if anything else like this happens. I'll ask you all one more time: did you have anything to do with the death of our brother?"

All three players shook their heads vigorously.

"Good," the dealer said as he began to deal the cards. "Let's finish the game."

13

Playing poker three-handed can move the game forward very quickly, but only if any one of the three players makes a move. For hand after hand, Eddie, Fat Man, and Green Shirt either folded to the big blind or called to see a cheap flop and then folded to a minimum bet once the cards were out on the table. There was no raising, no check-betting, and, by the time the blinds went up again, all three players found themselves with similar stacks of chips. On the next level, the big blind was two thousand four hundred—pretty much ten percent of their individual chip stacks. They all knew they had to stop playing safe and make a move if they were to stand a chance of surviving the night.

On the first hand of the level, Eddie was the big blind. Fat Man folded and Green Shirt called, after looking like he was thinking long and hard about a raise.

Has he got a pair? Eddie thought. *Maybe ace-king or ace-queen?*

Eddie looked at his cards: ace-six. He checked and the dealer dealt the flop, which came out four-eight-eight. The action was on Green Shirt. You didn't need to be an expert in body language to see that he hated the flop. He looked at his cards again, then at the flop. Then at his cards again. Then at his chip stack.

50

"Two-four," he said, and moved two thousand four hundred in chips over the line.

Eddie had a strong suspicion that Green Shirt's minimum bet was designed to shake him off the hand. The flop hadn't improved Green Shirt's hand, but he thought he had an opportunity to scoop up a few chips on the cheap.

Two can play that game, Eddie thought.

This was one of his favourite bluffing opportunities. A pair on the flop (eights with a four kicker in this case) significantly strengthened the hand belonging to anyone who already had an eight or a four, but it made everyone else reconsider their options, even if they were sitting on a pair of aces. Eddie had a single ace, which didn't put him in a bad position; he had the highest kicker if both of them only had the pair of eights. He weighed up his options.

I can't call. That would tell him I'm waiting for a specific card and he might hit the card he needs—the card he didn't get on the flop.

If I raise, I'll have to raise to around half my stack to have a chance of scaring him off.

If I go all-in, I'm putting everything at risk on a hunch.

I was the big blind and checked to see the flop. He's putting me on a wide range of hands so he could easily think I've got an eight or a four.

But that's what poker's about, isn't it?

No guts, no glory.

"All in," Eddie announced.

The lack of an instant call from Green Shirt gave Eddie confidence that he had read his opponent correctly. But after a few seconds of debate with himself, he called.

"On your backs," the dealer said.

51

They flipped their cards over and Eddie's heart sank. Green Shirt had been sitting on a pair of kings.

Son of a bitch, Eddie thought. He questioned the logic of his opponent not betting heavily or going all-in before the flop was dealt, but he knew why. They had all been playing so conservatively for the last few hands, an all-in or heavy bet before the flop would have scared Eddie off immediately. Green Shirt has been confident that he had the strongest hand but he was still playing for his life; he wanted to be certain that an ace didn't come out on the flop. He had put Eddie on an ace-kicker and he'd been right.

The dealer flipped over the turn card—a queen. That did nothing for either of them.

Then Eddie stood up, the way players do when they know they're about to be knocked out, even if there are cards still in the deck that will save them. This is a contentious move that goes against poker etiquette. Standing up and looking as if you're already walking away from the table when you've still got "outs" is seen as an attempt to tempt fate, to use your opponent's superstitions against them. Green Shirt immediately took exception to this.

"Wait a minute," he shouted, making a *stop* gesture with his hand to the dealer, who had the river card in his hand. "You've still got outs."

"Come on," Eddie said. "You've got me beat. Kings against my ace high. I'm a dead man. What do you care whether I stand up or not?"

"You've got outs. There are still aces in the deck." Green Shirt gestured to Fat Man. "Did you fold an ace?"

Fat Man shook his head.

"See? Still three aces in there. You're not dead yet, so sit down."

Eddie looked at Fat Man, who shrugged at him. The confident, hopeful look on Green Shirt's face that had appeared when he saw that his kings were way ahead had been replaced by a shaken, nervous stare. He was still gripping his pair of kings in his shaking hands.

Eddie sat down, expecting to stand up again for the last time just moments later. But he didn't have to. The river card was dealt.

Ace of spades.

The dealer went through the formality of announcing that "Aces win". Without missing a beat, Green Shirt stood up and leaned over the table, offering his hand to Eddie.

"Well played," Green Shirt said as they shook hands. "Good luck," were the last two words he spoke before he was dragged into the darkness behind him.

14

Now there were two players left and Eddie had a chip stack advantage of about two to one over Fat Man. The next set of hands went fold, fold, raise-fold, fold, raise-fold, fold, and fold. Eddie had tried raising with mid-strength hands a couple of times, but Fat Man was having none of it; he was waiting on his killer hand, ideally when he was the small blind.

He knew he had one chance left to get back in the game. There was no point in raising or calling if he thought he might have to fold to a raise—he wouldn't have enough chips to make a stand afterwards. He had to put his faith in two cards and go all-in before the flop. That came on the next hand.

Fat Man was the small blind and Eddie the big blind. Fat Man looked at his cards and immediately pushed his modest chip stack over the line. His voice cracked as he said "All in."

Eddie looked at his cards—red jacks. He closed his eyes and thought for a few seconds.

He hated playing jacks. It always looked like such a strong hand but he seemed to end up losing more hands than he won with those cards, especially if he was all-in before the flop. There's a good chance someone who goes all-in against jacks either has a stronger pair or at least one stronger card, if not two. He preferred going all-in with ace-king over jacks, even with its nickname of "Anna Kournikova"—*looks good, wins nothing.*

But he knew he had the chance to win the game and, most importantly, give himself a chance of surviving the night. Losing the hand would put him slightly behind in chip counts, but the blinds would be going up again soon so it felt like a good time to make the move.

"Call," he said.

"On your backs," the dealer ordered.

They turned their cards over and Eddie breathed a silent sigh of relief as he saw Fat Man's cards—a pair of tens. Fat Man muttered "Oh, shit" as he saw Eddie's cards.

"Jacks play tens," the dealer said.

I'm way ahead, Eddie thought. *Come on jacks, don't let me down this time!*

The way the dealer had been dealing the flop had been the same all night. He would discard one card—"burn one"—then deal three cards face down, one on top of another. He would then turn the pile of flop cards over, showing one card face up. Then in a single move, he would brush his hand over the cards, fanning them out to reveal the two hidden cards in one go. It's a fancy move that looks easy, but always results in ridicule for the dealer when he tries it during an amateur home game.

The dealer flipped his pile of three cards over and Eddie felt the blood drain from his face. The card on top was a ten.

Fat Man punched the air and shouted, "Yes!"

The dealer brushed his hand over the ten. When the move was complete, no one in the room—the players, the dealer, or the vampires that ringed the table in the darkness—could believe what they saw.

55

The flop came down ten-jack-jack. The dealer paused, mouth open, aghast at the sight before him. All around the room, Eddie heard low, disbelieving whistles from vampire teeth.

"Shit," Fat Man exclaimed, then said what everyone else was thinking. "I'm drawing dead."

He was right. He had trip-tens but he was facing up against quad-jacks.

Quad-jacks! Eddie thought. *On the flop!*

He'd never seen a hand like this before in his life. With a single movement of his hand, the dealer had saved Eddie's life, condemning the now-sobbing Fat Man to death. For no reason other than the formality of finishing the game, the dealer dealt a seven on the turn and a five on the river.

"Sorry," Eddie said as he offered his hand. Fat Man shook it.

"Don't worry about it," Fat Man said. "You made the right call."

Eddie was expecting to see Fat Man disappear into the darkness, dragged away by the clawing hands of his vampire sponsor. But this time, the victim was thrown forward. Fat Man screamed as he fell face-down onto the poker table, forcing him to eyeball his losing cards. The vampire behind him then leaned in with bared teeth and moved to sink them into his neck, but stopped. For a brief moment, the vampire turned to look at Eddie and said, "I was like you once. We all were."

Then he bit into Fat Man's neck. There was a spray of dark red mist, then the blood started to flow. The vampire sucked and lapped at the warm, pouring blood, but the flow from Fat Man's body was too strong and a pool started to form on the poker table, washing a tsunami of red over the white playing cards and engulfing the chips that lay scattered around Fat Man's body. The vampire's feeding frenzy ended and Fat Man's body remained on the table, his stony white face forever locked in a state of wide-eyed terror.

Eddie felt all alone. He was stuck in a room full of vampires. He'd played a game of poker for his life and won, but was there anything stopping them all from jumping him right now and feeding on his blood?

The dealer spoke. "Congratulations. You are the winner of our tournament. No doubt you are wondering what the prize is."

Eddie nodded, too scared to speak.

"I'll let your sponsor tell you," the dealer said, and got out of his seat. Raphael stalked round the table and sat down in his place.

"Eddie," he began, "what you have won is not a cash prize. It is not a World Series bracelet and you don't even have the right to tell your friends about how you won this tournament. After all, who would believe you? What you have won is the right to make a decision."

Eddie felt the tension in the room ease off ever so slightly. They didn't want to kill him—not immediately anyway. He'd already be dead if they did.

"What kind of decision?" he asked.

"Let's be clear about two things. One: when I backed you to play the World Series Main Event, you had nothing. You had blown your bankroll and you were probably only minutes away from mortgaging your plane ticket home or making another terrible decision that would eventually have got you killed, or at least in more trouble than you could handle with one of Vegas' many debt collectors. You were at rock bottom and had no choice. You are in this situation because you had nowhere else to go; you have no one to blame but yourself. We didn't put you in this situation—you did.

Two: tonight, you have learned one of the world's great secrets. Yes, vampires do exist and you have met them. Some of what you think you know about us is true—the myths and legends have their roots in the truth. Our physical weaknesses are exploited by ultra-violet light, silver, and a number of poisons. One of the players at this table knew that; he was an undercover agent of a group called the Brotherhood, which thinks they will kill us all. But make no mistake, we will prevail. There are hundreds of thousands of us all over the world—maybe even millions—and we survive under the radar of normal society, but we hide in plain sight. We have influence over all major international organisations and, like anyone else, we seek entertainment.

"Poker is ideal. Thousands of people gathered in one place, disappearing one by one without notice by the other people left in the room. And best of all, no sunlight, even during July in Vegas. We play, we make money, we stake other players—no pun intended—and we only reveal our true selves when we need to. Also—and this is where you have to make a decision—we recruit others to add to our numbers."

Eddie shifted in his chair. He had a terrible feeling he knew where this conversation was going.

"You are a great poker player, Eddie. You can read your opponent, which is why I can tell you know what I am about to ask you. You have two choices. The first is simple: you submit to me and allow me to feed on your blood. You will be no different from your opponents tonight: you will die."

And the second choice? Eddie's face asked.

"Your second choice is so much more beautiful. Join us. Become one of us. Travel the world, play in the biggest poker tournaments, find new talent for us, and enjoy our fabulous wealth.

58

Indulge all of your human fantasies and discover so many more. I offer you immortality."

Eddie closed his eyes and thought for a moment, then gave Raphael his answer.

15
Four months later

In November, the World Series of Poker circus returns to Las Vegas. Two weeks of play in July come to an end when there are just nine players left. The tournament then goes on hiatus until November, when the final table plays out. All the players return to a single table with the same chips counts they walked away with in the summer, only this time some of them are sitting down wearing the badges of new sponsors, who have paid them more than they stand to earn in prize money unless they finish first or second.

As with any major tournament, especially those that are scrutinised under the TV lights, the main action is in the side games. While the November Nine were playing out the final table, the poker rooms of every casino up and down the strip were packed with high stakes tournaments and cash games. Every few hours, millions of dollars changed hands and the casinos took their cut.

The mix of characters was astonishing to the tourists. Spotty kids dressed in hoodies and sporting oversized, over-priced headphones barely past their twenty-first birthdays rubbed shoulders with greats of the game and Hollywood stars with too much spare time and huge amounts of money in the bank. No tournament of note had a buy-in less than ten thousand dollars and the entry-level cash games set the big blinds at one thousand dollars and required a bank roll of at least twenty-five thousand dollars before a player could take a seat at the table. Whether a player was an actor on ten million a movie or a Scandinavian online pro who played twelve tables at once from the comfort of his bedroom, it didn't matter who you were. If you had the money, you were guaranteed a seat and, unless you wanted a shot at the top-level cash games, the money brought you no advantage. A poker table is one of society's greatest level playing fields.

One of the thousands of high stakes players that found themselves moving from table to table during this week in November was Andrea Di Maria. A year ago, the twenty-six year old Spanish Andie—or señorita_fish as she was known online—finished tenth in the World Series of Poker Main Event, missing out on the final table but walking away from the Rio with a bankroll of almost one million dollars. Unfortunately for her, that was the beginning of her problems.

She had been grinding out a decent living playing poker both online and in major live events, but things changed when she won the World Series of Poker Europe Main Event and found herself a million euros richer. Like many professional players, she attracted the attention of agents, publicists, and moneyed individuals who wanted to stake her in major tournaments. After much deliberation, she had decided to sign with an agent to manage the opportunities that were flooding her way, sacrificing ten percent of her future income to have someone manage her endorsements and negotiate terms with all the people and organisations who were throwing themselves at her.

All was going well until she finished tenth in the Main Event. It was only at that point that she discovered her manager had got too many backers for her entry into all twenty World Series events she entered that year. He had a secret gambling problem and, to cover his losses, he was offering out too much of a stake to potential backers. Her winnings that summer amounted to around $1.5 million, but her manager had sold stakes in her winnings to backers of one hundred and fifty percent. For the Main Event that cost $10,000 to enter, he had sold ten percent stakes in her winnings to thirteen different people, using the leftover $3,000 to pay off his own debts. Her backers now wanted repayments totalling just over two million dollars. Her manager quickly disappeared and, ever since, she had been pleading with everyone to give her time to pay them back.

But the last year had not been kind to her. After failing to make the money levels of any major tournament and a bad run playing high stakes online, she found herself having to drop down the stakes and grind out a profit combining a meagre existence with a massive volume of low-stakes games against amateurs. Yes, she was making money, but it could take another two or three years to get back to where she needed to be and, all the while, her backers were threatening to increase their interest charges. So she had rolled up all of her winnings over the last year and decided to take her bankroll to Vegas for November Nine week, looking for a jackpot.

But word had got round that she was in town and her backers tracked her down. If she could afford to get on a plane to Vegas and stay on the strip, she could pay off her debt quicker than she had been doing so far. In reality, she had taken the desert bus and was staying in one of the worst motels in town, nowhere near the strip. That meant nothing to her backers—she'd been given new deadlines, the first being the end of the week.

Now she was one of four players left at a table where the price of a seat was seventy-five thousand dollars. It had been almost all of her bankroll, but this was her chance. If she finished third, she would get her money back. Finish second and she would try to buy herself some time. Win the tournament and she would finally be back in the black.

There was an audience around the table, all eager to see who would win the game—the movie star, the ex-tennis pro, the online kid, or that girl from Spain who used to be a good player—and many hands had been greeted with whoops and cheers from the baying crowd.

Andrea was on the dealer button as the dealer dealt the cards. She was the marginal short stack but that didn't worry her—the game had been quick so far and the blinds weren't making much of a dent in her stack on each rotation. All she had to do was keep her head and wait for opportunities to increase her stack.

The online kid to her right looked at his cards and, without missing a beat, went all in. The crowd let out a collective "Ooooh!"

The action was on Andrea, but she paid little attention to the kid's announcement. He had been playing fast and loose for the whole game. He was clearly used to playing online and hadn't adjusted his game to playing in a live tournament. By her estimate, he had been involved in four out of every five hands and the range of hands he played was pretty much any two cards. His chip stack had varied wildly thought the game and, while he had Andrea covered, she suspected she had him beat as soon as she looked at her cards.

Ace of spades, ace of hearts.

American Airlines.

Bullets.

Pocket rockets.

She laid her cards face down and tried her best to look like she was considering playing a weaker hand than she had. The tennis player and the movie star hadn't looked at their cards yet, so she couldn't gauge whether they were planning to fold, call, or raise the kid's all-in. In any normal situation she would have preferred to be all-in against just one other player, but she knew she had the kid beat—he was probably trying to knock her out on a crowd-pleasing two-seven off-suit—and she wanted to drag one of the other two players into the mix. Winning this hand wouldn't knock anyone out, but she had the chance to massively increase her chip stack and put one or two players on the brink of going out.

She looked directly ahead at the dealer and announced that she was all-in, then pushed her chip stack over the line. Her move was met by another rumbling "Ooooooh" by the crowd.

The tennis player looked at his cards, looked at his stack, looked at the movie star's stack—the biggest at the table—and announced that he was going all-in too.

The movie star checked his cards and, without taking a breath, said "Call."

The crowd went insane. The online kid stood up with a shit-eating grin on his face and shook his head at some of his friends in the crowd, reaching over behind the barrier and exchanging high-fives. Andrea knew she had read him perfectly—he had played terrible cards and would be way behind the other three players when they turned their cards over.

With everyone all-in, it took the dealer a minute or two to arrange the chip stacks in the correct piles according to the main pot and side pots. The tension was at breaking point when he said, "On your backs."

The online kid showed his cards first. Andrea had been wrong, but not by much. He didn't have the worst possible hand— he had the second worst. Two-eight off-suit.

Andrea turned over her aces and the crowd erupted. The kid tapped the table in respect.

The tennis player shook his head, sighed, and turned over a pair of kings. The noise from the crowd turned up a notch, but it was cranked right up to eleven when the movie star showed his cards.

Ace of clubs, ace of diamonds.

Andrea and the movie star exchanged looks. Her look said, "God help me." His look said, "Sorry."

She was now at a massive disadvantage. With no more aces in the deck and her potential winnings being cut in two, she was relying on their aces holding all the way to the river or hitting a flush of hearts or spades. This was not good at all.

The dealer dealt the flop. Nine. King. King.

The movie star, the online kid, and Andrea all hung their heads, but none more so than Andrea. The dealer paused for a few seconds, allowing the situation to sink in among the crowd, then someone shouted, "Holy shit, they're all drawing dead!"

The tennis player had hit four of a kind on the flop. With no aces left and not enough cards to make a straight flush, the aces held by Andrea and the movie star were worthless. Given the chip counts before the hand, it was now between the movie star and the kid to see who finished in second place.

Andrea didn't want to find out. It didn't matter—she was out in fourth place. No prize money. No hope.

She got out of her chair and pushed her way through the crowd, with "Tough break" and "Well played" ringing in her ears. Their consolation meant nothing to her—her life was surely over. Her bankroll was gone. She had nothing to show for the last year of her life apart from spiralling debt, insomnia, and the very likely prospect of a contract being put out on her life.

Andrea trudged zombie-like through the maze of gaming tables and bleeping machines and made for the blazing sunshine outside. Before she reached the casino's exit, she felt a hand on her shoulder.

"Miss Di Maria?"

She spun round and found herself face-to-face with a man in his mid-twenties, dressed in a black suit with an open-neck white shirt.

"That was quick," she said with a sigh. "Have they sent you to collect the money already? You can tell them I lost. I've got no money for them. I'll be in room 103 at the Safari Motel if they want to send someone to kill me."

"I think you are mistaken, Miss Di Maria. I am not here on behalf of the men you owe money to."

"So what do you want?"

"You're a good poker player, Miss Di Maria. You've been on a bad run."

"How do you know? Do I know you?"

"You don't know me but I know of you. I've been watching you play the whole time you've been in Vegas. I'm a talent scout and I want to make you an offer."

"A talent scout for who?"

66

"Some people who can make the people you owe money to go away. Let me buy you a drink and I'll tell you more, Miss Di Maria."

She thought for a moment, then realised she had no better option in her future.

"Okay," she said, "but stop calling me Miss. Call me Andrea, or Andie."

"Of course, Andrea."

"And what's your name?"

"My name is Eddie Nelson," he said, holding out his hand. She shook it.

"Follow me, please," Eddie said, leading her back into the darkness of the casino.

I hope you enjoyed reading Drawing Dead. If you did, I would be eternally grateful if you were to write a short review on Amazon or Goodreads, or find me online and tell me what you think.

You may also like my latest novel, a conspiracy thriller called *One Day in Gitmo Nation*.

In the near future, the world stands on the edge of global governance. In less than twenty-four hours, the lives of seven different people will be forever entwined in a global conspiracy that will result in the President's assassination.

To find out more, visit
www.scottamckenzie.com

Or turn the page to read a sample from the first chapter...

One Day in Gitmo Nation

Chapter 1: The Watch List

1

The day of the president's assassination began like any other.

Terminal nine at JFK International Airport was as busy as ever. The summer was drawing to a close and the check-in desks were obscured from view by long queues of passengers snaking their way up, down, left, and right into any available space. The tired and frustrated masses inched along the first of many queues they would find themselves standing in before they eventually reached their destination, even more tired and frustrated than they were at the beginning of the day.

At just after five o'clock in the morning, the automatic entrance doors opened and Andy Conway stepped across the threshold into the air-conditioned terminal, dressed in comfortable cargo pants, a hooded top loaded with pockets, and slip-on sneakers: the uniform of a seasoned traveller. He was emotionally prepared for a familiar kind of discomfort. His knuckles turned white as he gripped the handle of his wheeled suitcase and dragged it over to the screens that told him which check-in queue he was now forced to endure.

From the first time he took a flight when he was eight years old and his father nearly got into a fight at a baggage carousel with a drunken British tourist who refused to get out of the way when his bag went past, he had always considered airports to be the places that bring out the worst in humanity. In a place where thousands of people gather together, standing on the threshold of a week or two away from the hassles of day-to-day life, the reality is a giant room of queuing, stripping down, and answering questions barked by a jobsworth with a badge. The sound of arguing couples and screaming children filled the sterile air as Andy took his place at the back of his check-in line.

He edged his way through the queue and listened to music to drown out the noise of the general public. Avoiding eye contact or the chance of sharing an awkward moment with any fellow traveller he might find himself sitting next to on the long flight ahead, he cast his eyes round the check-in hall and saw dozens of people doing exactly the same thing. But he noticed the most interesting thing just in front of him in the queue.

The name 'Andy Conway' was written on an old, well-travelled baggage tag stuck to the suitcase belonging to the man standing in front of him. Not only did they have the same name, their appearances were similar too: similar height, greying brown hair, and a handsome face, if Andy did say so himself. He raised an eyebrow at the thought of bumping into someone with the same name as him and thought no more of it.

After a half-hour wait, Andy found himself standing at the front of the roped-off check-in queue. There were two desks ahead of him at which two separate lines had formed. Andy chose to stand back, intending to subvert Murphy's Law, which always came into play when choosing a queue at supermarket checkouts. He heard a grumble from behind.

"Excuse me," exclaimed a female voice in a tone that was a long-distance flight away from civil, accompanied by a tap on the shoulder. Andy turned his head only far enough to see that he was being addressed by an irate woman standing in front of her mousey husband who was holding their sleeping toddler in his arms. They were dressed in what Andy suspected was their Sunday best: a painfully obvious attempt to get an upgrade, which would surely not work and they would then be destined to spend the rest of the day adjusting their uncomfortable clothes while they were crammed into their economy seats.

He'd never met these people before, but he'd met their type countless times: once-a-year travellers who think they deserve special treatment just because that's what they usually get in their own little bubble. Andy was a regular flier and knew that those rules didn't apply in an airport. If you don't hand over your hard-earned cash for special treatment, it's every man for himself, locked in a massive structure together where no one cares who you are. You are just another schmuck in a queue and you will be treated with the same contempt as the next schmuck.

Andy raised an eyebrow and let out a grunt that said, *What do you want?*

The lady took a deep breath before speaking with a tone that clearly said, *I can't believe you don't know why I'm angry.*

"There are two lines here. Which desk are you waiting for?" she demanded with crossed arms. Andy knew she would be tapping her toe as well, but he couldn't bring himself to give her any more of his attention than a glance over his shoulder. Her husband was maintaining his silence, something Andy assumed he'd learned to do after a married life filled with futile protests.

Andy removed his ear buds and waved his hand in a gesture toward each desk, where their fellow passengers were going through the check-in procedure. "Whichever one's free next."

73

He resisted adding "We're not in the supermarket, lady".

"You're not supposed to do that. You need to join a queue." He had predicted she would say that as soon as he felt the tap on his shoulder.

"This is the fairest way."

Before the argument could continue any further, a desk became free. For the second time that morning, Andy Conway breathed a sigh of relief and took a step forward.

2

"Did you pack your luggage yourself?" the pretty female check-in assistant asked.

Just like every time he went through the laborious check-in procedure, Andy bit his lip and answered "Yes, I did," rather than "No, a nice man with dark skin and a long black beard offered to do it for me."

While the check-in assistant was tagging his suitcase and checking his passport, out of the corner of his eye he saw the woman who had been behind him in the queue approach the next desk with her family in tow. Within seconds, she was demanding an upgrade, but the assistant behind the desk refused to award any freebies. With the thought that he might find himself sitting next to his latest nemesis or, worse than that, her soon-to-be-screaming child, he asked his assistant how much an upgrade would cost.

"Since you are a frequent flier, the cost will be fifty dollars," was the answer and, without batting an eyelid, Andy Conway reached into his pocket and slapped five ten-dollar bills on the desk.

"Sold!" he announced, with far too much enthusiasm for anyone to summon before six in the morning.

74

"Okay, let me just find you a seat," she said, taking the money without looking his way. "That's weird," she said, after tapping at the keyboard and doing a double take at her screen.

"Is there a problem?"

The assistant shook her head as if blanking an occurrence of déjà vu from her mind. "No, nothing to worry about."

She gave Andy his boarding pass and luggage ticket and wished him a good flight. Andy threw his carry-on bag over his shoulder and made his way past the family he was glad to be avoiding for the rest of the flight. He wondered if the check-in assistant had seen that the other Andy Conway had been booked on the same flight. He then wondered if that also meant his namesake was also sitting in first class. He gave another internal chuckle at the thought of sitting next to the other Andy Conway. He'd never met anyone with his name before.

Andy's pulse quickened as he approached passport control. Even though he was certain of his complete innocence of the slightest wrong-doing (he'd never had so much as a parking ticket), he always felt like he was walking through passport control or customs with 'I am a terrorist' tattooed on his forehead. He walked past the passengers who had forgotten they couldn't take any more than 100ml of liquid onboard the plane and were throwing away their industrial-size bottles of shampoo. He always wondered why people would bother taking such massive bottles away with them if they were only going away for two weeks at most. In the distance, he heard a man shout "Don't touch my junk, bro!" followed by a commotion, but he was too far back in the line to see what was going on.

After another eternity standing in line, he walked up to the only passport control desk that was manned (or wo-manned in this case) and handed over his passport and boarding pass.

"Where are you going?" she barked at him.

"Italy," he said.

"This ticket says Rome on it."

"Rome is in Italy," he replied in a deadpan tone.

The assistant swiped his passport under the scanner and stopped to look at the screen for a second. She then took a pen out of her shirt pocket and scribbled a capital F on his boarding pass. She looked past Andy and gave a 'come here' wave with her hand to someone behind him. Andy turned round to find himself confronted with the biggest TSA guard he'd ever seen and couldn't help but notice the gun on his belt.

"What's going on?" Andy asked, with the onset of panic in his mind betrayed by the crack in his voice.

"Please go with the guard, sir," she ordered and handed his passport and boarding pass to the guard.

"What's going on?" he asked again.

"Please come with me, sir," the guard said very calmly, "We don't want to make a scene."

3

Andy found himself standing in a bare, well-lit room, about ten feet square, with a desk against the far wall. Andy's fears doubled as he looked round the cramped room.

No windows. No cameras. No one knew he was here and, more importantly, he didn't know why he was here. The guard slammed the door behind them.

"What's going on?" he asked for a third time. For a third time, he received no answer.

The door opened and a man with three stripes on his brown shirt walked in. Without exchanging any words, the guard handed Andy's passport and boarding pass to the man with the stripes and stood to attention in the corner of the room to await orders from his superior. The man rifled through the passport, examining the archive of immigration stamps in great detail.

"Your name is Andrew Conway," the officer said, and only looked up when he didn't get a response within the time he was expecting. "I asked you a question. Is your name Andrew Conway?"

Andy hadn't realised it was a question. "Yes, my name is Andrew Conway."

"You go to Europe a lot."

"Yes, it's with business, I'm a—"

"Silence! I didn't ask you a question."

Andy frowned and maintained a confused silence. After another minute of flicking through his passport, the officer barked at him again.

"Open up the bag."

Andy put his bag on the desk and started to open it.

"Not you!" the officer shouted. He looked at the guard and repeated his order.

With the precision of a bomb disposal expert, the guard unzipped the bag and peeked inside. He carefully picked the items out of the bag and placed them on the desk, one by one.

Andy suddenly realised the contents of his bag might look a bit suspect to the casual observer, never mind these Nazis from the Transportation Security Administration. He was an engineer for

Synergy Services, a multinational IT corporation. He was required to travel with his laptop and a wide range of tools and spare parts, which he tried to tell the officer, but was cut off mid-sentence with another shout of "Silence!"

The officer paid no attention to the cables and other technological paraphernalia that came out of the bag until the last item emerged. Very carefully, the guard lifted a bottle of 7UP out of the bag. Andy realised he'd forgotten about it, and the stringent rules about taking liquids on planes meant that anything outside the rules was immediately treated as a potential explosive device.

"What have we here?" the officer asked, delivering his line like a prosecutor might when presenting the damning piece of evidence to the jury.

4

The other Andy Conway sat down with a coffee and three newspapers. He hadn't dared to go through passport control yet, instead opting to see what alerts, if any, his checking-in had raised. The table he chose gave him a good view of the line of travellers waiting to go through passport control and the army of guards patrolling the retail monument that doubled as an airport terminal. As far as he could tell, the security staff were all going about their business as normal.

He let his coffee cool down as he flicked through the pages of the broadsheets. His pulse slowed as he turned more and more pages. There were no reports about experimental research, certainly nothing he was involved in. There was nothing about missing persons, certainly not from the company he worked for. And there was nothing about the President, certainly nothing other than the fact that President Green had attended the concert by teen singing sensation Anna Indiana at Madison Square Garden last night, and his children had been conspicuous by their absence.

The cappuccino went down in four large gulps. He just wanted the caffeine to keep him alert long enough to get onto the plane and off the ground. After that, he was planning to sleep all the way to Europe. Sleep was a commodity he'd been short of recently. The world of scientific and political scandals doesn't sleep, so neither did he, and there had never been a scientific or political scandal like this before.

He looked at his watch. His flight would be taking off in just over an hour. *It's now or never*, he thought. *If you don't go through passport control, you can't get out of the country that wants you dead.*

The other Andy Conway got to his feet and joined the queue to go through passport control. There was no need for him to worry, though. Little did he know that another Andy Conway had already gone through passport control. Little did he know that the software which alerted the passport control officer to write a capital F on the boarding pass deleted the flag once the first person with the flagged name had been identified. Without this in mind, the other Andy Conway had his passport and boarding pass returned to him by the officer and cruised through to the departure lounge.

Coincidentally, the IT company that created the bug-ridden passport control software was Synergy Services, the company that the unfortunate Andy Conway worked for. Had both Andy Conways known this fact, it's likely that one of them would have found it funnier than the other.

5

"It's a bottle of 7UP," Andy said.

"What's it doing in there?" the man with the stripes asked.

"I forgot about it. I bought it last night on the way home from work and must have left it in there when I packed the rest of my things."

The guard thrust the bottle into Andy's face. "Drink it," he said.

"What, all of it?"

"No. Just taste it so we know it's not toxic."

Andy took the bottle in his hands and twisted the cap, which cracked the seal as he opened it. He pointed this out to the officer but the man with stripes didn't care.

"Drink it," he repeated.

Andy swallowed a mouthful and waited a few seconds to prove that he wasn't about to keel over and die. The officer grabbed the bottle out of Andy's hand and sniffed the contents, then handed it to the guard who did the same. They gave each other a nod. The guard grabbed the cap out of Andy's hand and screwed it onto the bottle.

"Put everything back in your bag," the officer said. "We'll be back."

They slammed the door behind them, leaving Andy alone in the room. He was shell-shocked. Was this really happening to him? Surely they couldn't think he was a terrorist? Then it dawned on him.

They must think I'm the other Andy Conway. Who the hell is that guy?

He stuffed everything back in his bag and, after a few minutes of pacing round the tiny room, he sat down on the desk. He checked his watch. The plane would take off in less than an hour, which meant he only had about twenty minutes to board the plane before the gate was due to close.

The more he looked at his watch, the quicker the second hand seemed to tick round. He stood up and paced some more. He put his hands in his pockets and realised his captors hadn't taken his mobile phone from him. It had a decent signal, so he connected to the internet and began some amateur detective work.

He searched Google for 'Andrew Conway', which returned 14,000 results. He refined the search to 'Andrew Conway New York', which cut the results down to 489 results. He chose the first link, which took him to a *New York Times* article from a couple of years ago about a visit to a research lab in New York by Senator Harry Green, who at the time was in the running to be the Democratic nominee for the next year's presidential election. Andy scrolled down the page and found his name.

Head of research Dr. Andrew Conway hosted the tour of the Alset research facilities, which have taken great leaps forward in the cloning of mammals in the last five years.

6

In the corridor outside, the officer told the guard to wait by the door and let no one in or out. He marched down the corridor and went into another empty room, then took out his phone and called the number he had saved in his contacts list under the name 'Escalation'.

The officer hadn't called that number for over six months. It had been a long time since he'd seen a boarding pass with an F written on it. Why did he have to delay this poor schmuck before his flight? It was obvious to him that this guy had done nothing wrong, but there was a procedure to follow and the people who wrote this procedure were the ones who could make or break your career. Or make or break your life.

The gruff voice on the other end picked up the call almost immediately.

"Yeah?" he growled.

"It's Officer Mills from JFK. We've picked up a flagged passenger."

"What's his name?"

"Andrew Conway."

"Really? Give me a second."

The officer heard some tapping at a keyboard in the background, followed by a chuckle.

"Has he given you any trouble?" the man on the other end asked.

"No. None at all. Right now he's sitting alone in one of our holding rooms, shitting his pants."

"Let him go."

"Yes, sir."

"One more thing," the gruff voice said, "are any of your officers taking the same flight as that passenger?"

"Yes, sir. A routine—"

"Get them off the plane. Now. But make sure that guy gets on the plane. Use force if you have to." With that, the man on the other end hung up.

7

Andy sneaked his mobile phone back into his pocket as soon as his captors walked through the door. Something in their demeanour had changed. Andy could tell they weren't interested in him anymore.

"You can go," the officer said.

"What was all this about?" Andy asked.

"Our mistake. We're very sorry for any inconvenience."

"I think I know what the problem is. There's another man on my flight with the same name as me."

"You'd better go if you're going to catch your flight, sir."

"But ..."

"Have a nice day, sir."

The officer stood aside and beckoned Andy to leave, which he promptly did, but he still had the thought nagging his mind that he was about to get on a plane with someone the TSA needed to speak to on board.

The guard escorted Andy back down the corridor, through the door at the end, and past passport control. With an insincere "Have a nice flight," the guard left Andy standing in the departure lounge. Andy checked the departure boards and then his watch. With ten minutes left to board, he walked over to a vending machine to get a bottle of Hero-Cola and made his way toward the gate, only to be confronted by representatives from Duo-Cola giving out free bottles of a new soft drink.

Upon reaching the gate, he joined yet another queue of passengers waiting to board the plane and he saw his namesake at the front of the line.

Should I go and speak to him? Andy thought. *Should I ask him if he was interrogated as well? Maybe I should report him.*

Andy looked around him and saw a TSA officer standing at the end of the moving walkway. It was the officer who had questioned him just minutes earlier.

Andy left his place in the queue, knowing that if he had to rejoin it, he would have to go to the back. People were always so precious about their place in a queue but it wasn't as if the plane was going to take off without everyone in the queue, was it?

The officer took a step toward Andy as he approached. "Yes, sir, can I help you?" he asked. There was no recognition in his eyes. He was staring at Andy as if they had never met before, as if he hadn't been interrogating him just minutes earlier.

"The man I was telling you about—the other Andy Conway—is in the queue over there. He's going to get on my plane."

"I'm sure I don't know what you're talking about, sir," he replied, with a blank expression on his face.

"What? You were looking for someone called Andy Conway. The man you were looking for is over there in the queue. He's about to get on the plane."

"I'm afraid you're mistaken, sir." The officer's tone of voice changed and was Andy could see the recognition in his eyes. "Now, let me be clear about this: return to the line and board the plane."

With that, the officer squared his shoulders and seemed to grow a few inches taller.

"But, he's just there. Get the crew to check his passport; you'll see I'm not lying."

"I don't think you're a liar, sir." The officer left that last comment hanging in the air, all the while staring into Andy's eyes.

Andy realised his protests would get him nowhere. "Whatever's going on here, I don't like it," he said. "I'm going to take a later flight."

As Andy took his first step, the officer grabbed his arm and pulled him back. The officer didn't let go and tightened his grip until Andy could feel the blood being cut off from his hand.

"Sir," the officer growled, "may I remind you that knives are prohibited items in the cabin of an airplane."

Now Andy was really confused. "Knives? What do you mean?"

"I'd merely like to remind you that knives are prohibited on board any airplanes taking off from any U.S. airport. Knives like this one."

Concealing his actions from everyone else in the departure lounge, the officer made sure that Andy saw him take a Stanley knife out of his pocket and extend the blade.

"Now turn around, forget everything you've seen and heard, and get on the fucking plane."